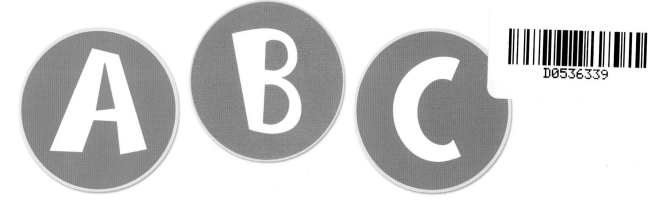

ABC

A Family Alphabet Book

Bobbie Combs

illustrated by Desiree Keane & Brian Rappa

Two Lives Publishing

UNIVERSITY OF NV LAS VEGAS
CURRICULUM MATERIALS LIBRARY
101 EDUCATION
LAS VEGAS, NV 89154
WITHDRAWN

D0536339

Published by
Two Lives Publishing
508 North Swarthmore Avenue
Ridley Park, PA 19078

Visit our website: www.twolives.com

Copyright © 2000 by Bobbie Combs
Illustrations copyright © 2000 by Desiree Keane and Brian Rappa
Book production by Kids At Our House

All rights reserved. No part of this book may be reproduced or transmitted in any form or by any means,
electronic or mechanical, including photocopying, recording, or by any information storage and retrieval system,
without the written permission of the Publisher, except where permitted by law.

ISBN: 0-9674468-1-3

Library of Congress Cataloging-in-Publication Data
00-108093

2 3 4 5 6 7 8 9 10

Printed in China

For my one-of-a-kind family:
thank you for your unconditional love.
— B.C.

For my family who has always supported me
and for Brian to whom I'll always be drawn.
—D.K.

For the rest of my life to start and end
with my future wife, Desiree.
—B.R.

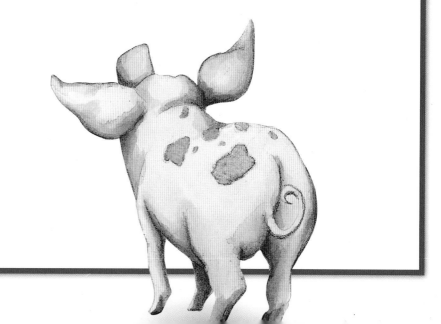

A is for awake.

Every morning, I am the first one awake in our house.

B is for book.

Our moms read our favorite book to us at bedtime.

C is for cookies.

Both of my dads know how to make great chocolate chip cookies.

D is for ducks.

Every weekend, we feed the **ducks** in the park.

E

is for eggs.

On Sunday mornings, we eat scrambled eggs for breakfast.

F is for family.

Everyone in our family loves to play baseball.

G is for garden.

My moms like it when I help them work in the garden.

H is for hugs.

Our dads give us big hugs when they pick us up from school.

is for ice cream.

I like vanilla ice cream,
but my moms like chocolate best.

J is for jacket.

I put on my red jacket when it is cold outside.

K is for kitten.

Our new **kitten** is the smallest member of our family.

L is for lunch.

We always pack a picnic lunch when my moms take me to the beach.

M is for moon.

In the summertime, we sit on our porch and look at the moon.

N is for night.

I take a bath every **night** before I go to bed.

O

is for overalls.

I always wear my **overalls** when my dads take us to the playground.

P is for penguins.

My moms like to take me to the aquarium to look at the penguins.

Q is for quilt.

I have a blue and orange quilt on my bed.

R

is for rainbow.

Sometimes after it rains, we can see a **rainbow** in the sky.

S

is for snow.

In the wintertime, I can write
my name in the **snow**.

T is for toys.

My friends and I always share our toys with each other.

U is for umbrella.

My pink umbrella keeps me dry when it is raining.

V is for vegetables.

When we go grocery shopping, my moms buy lots of **vegetables**.

W is for wagon.

Sometimes I ride in my wagon when my dads take me for a walk.

X is for xylophone.

I know how to play all of my favorite songs on my xylophone.

Y is for yard.

In the autumn, our dog chases the leaves outside in our yard.

Z is for zoo.

Our family loves to visit the animals at the petting ZOO.

Bobbie Combs is a children's book consultant and one of the owners
of Two Lives Publishing. She lives in Philadelphia, Pennsylvania.

This is the first full color collaboration between Desiree Keane and Brian Rappa.
Brian is a graduate of Philadelphia's Hussian School of Art, and Desiree holds a BFA
from Rosemont College. Both Desiree and Brian live in New Jersey.